I0682945

# THE SPACE MERCHANTS

—

*Kiss The Dirt*

ALR016

*Published by*

**Aqualamb**

The Space Merchants are:
Aileen Brophy – Bass and Vox
Michael Guggino – Vox and Guitars
Carter Logan – Drums and Percussion
Ani Monteleone – Vox and Keys

Produced by James Brown
Recorded and Mixed by James Brown
at Terminus Studios, NYC and The Union, New York
Engineering Assistance by Daniel Avila

Mastered by Adam Gonsalves at Telegraph Audio, Portland, OR

Additional Keys recorded by Aaron W. Jacobsen
at Green Fort Studio, Brooklyn

Cover artwork by Brualio Amado
Graphic novel story by Joshua Ray Stephens and Michael Guggino
Illustrated by Joshua Ray Stephens
🌐 thursdaycity.com    📷 jehosephatsunrays
Additional design production by Eric Palmerlee

aqualamb.org

# CONTENTS

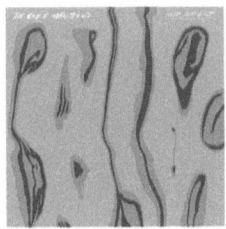

The music for this release
can be downloaded
via the link below:

http://aqualamb.org/016

KISS THE DIRT

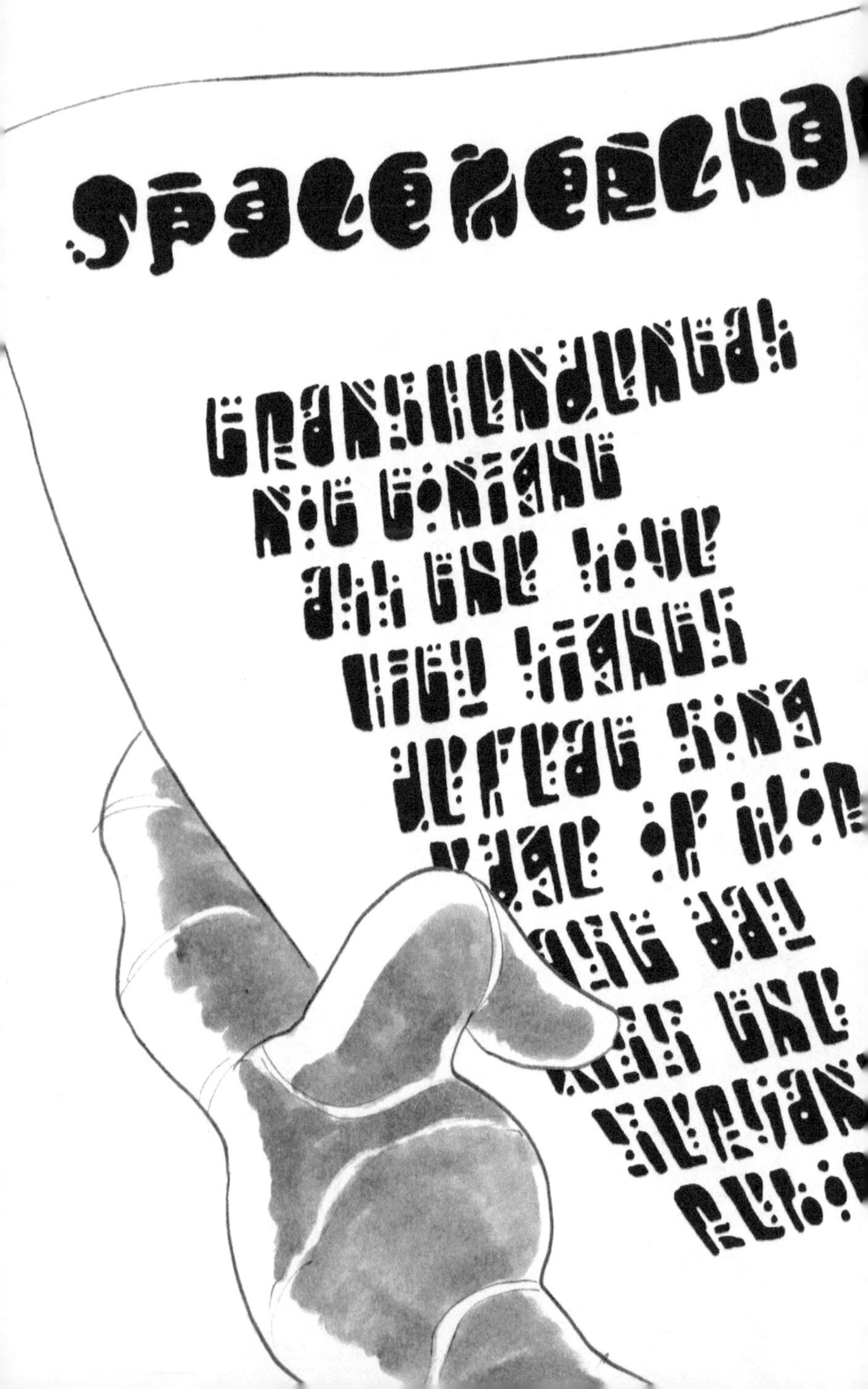

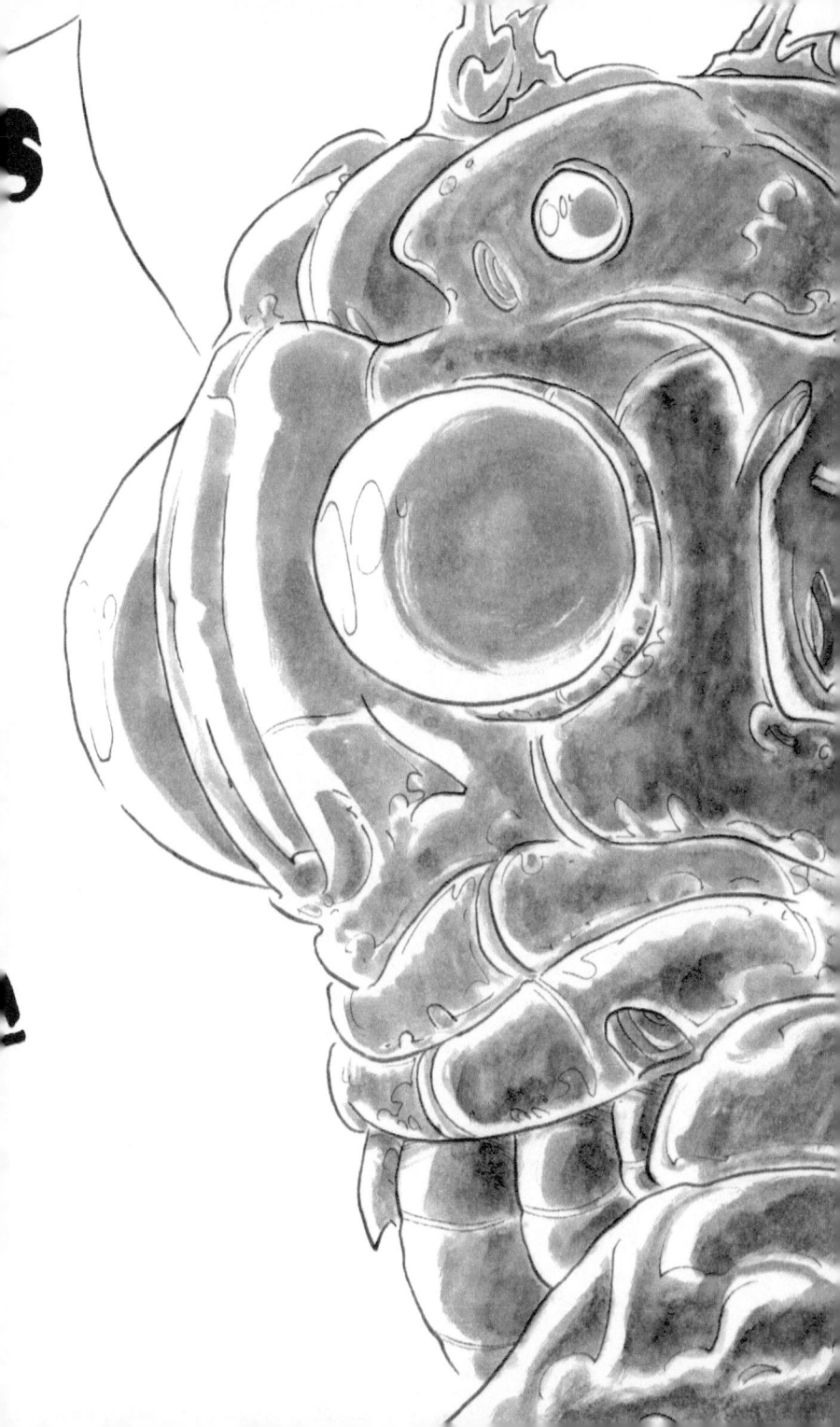

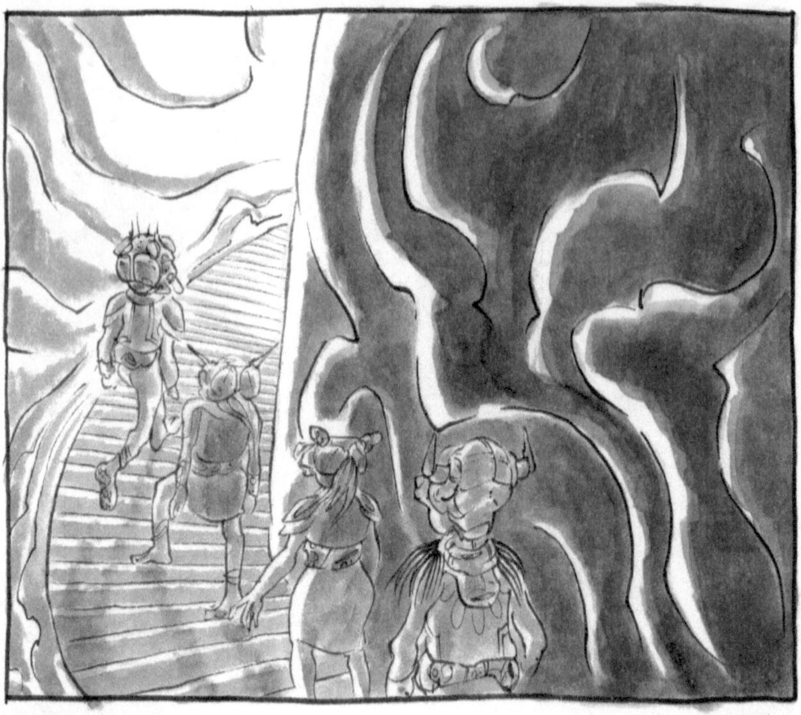

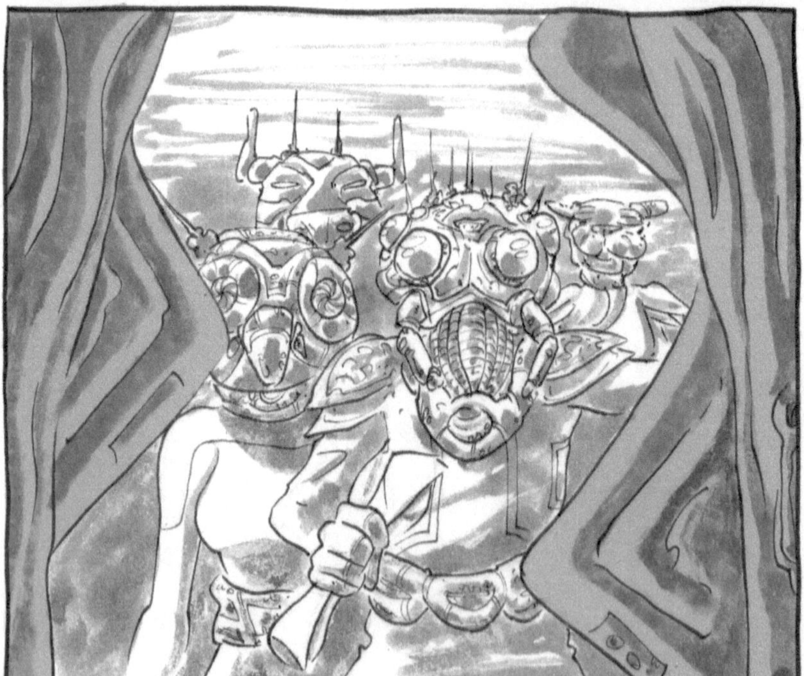

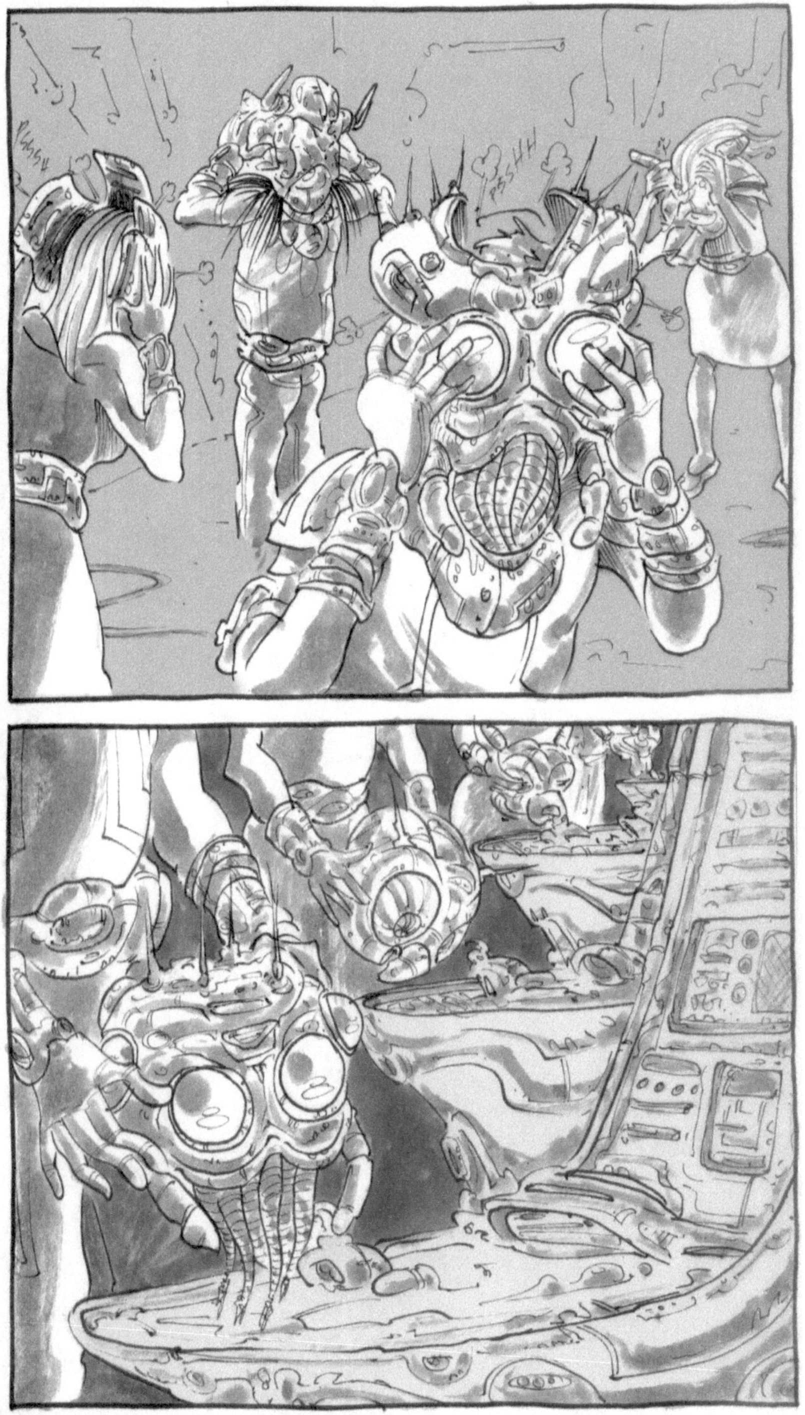
PSSHH

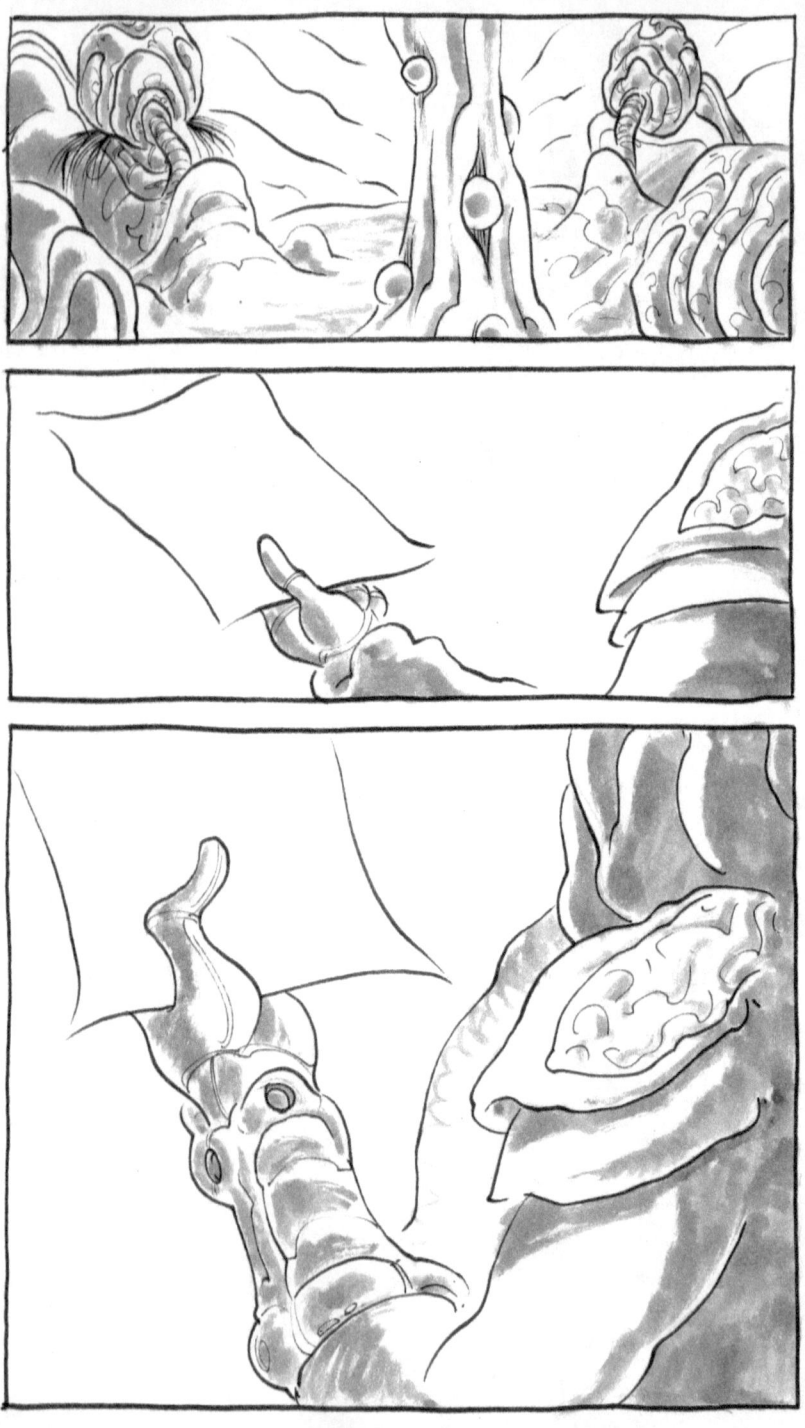

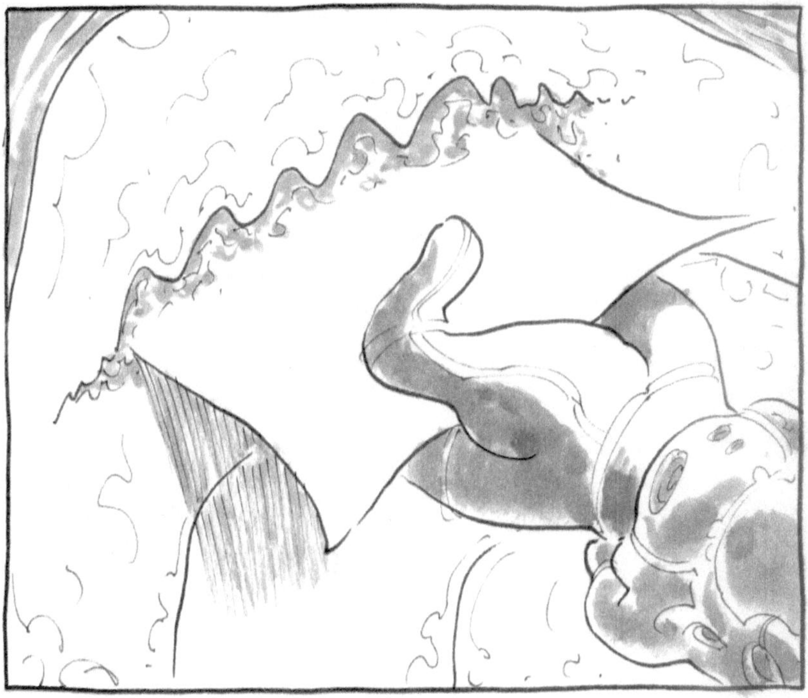

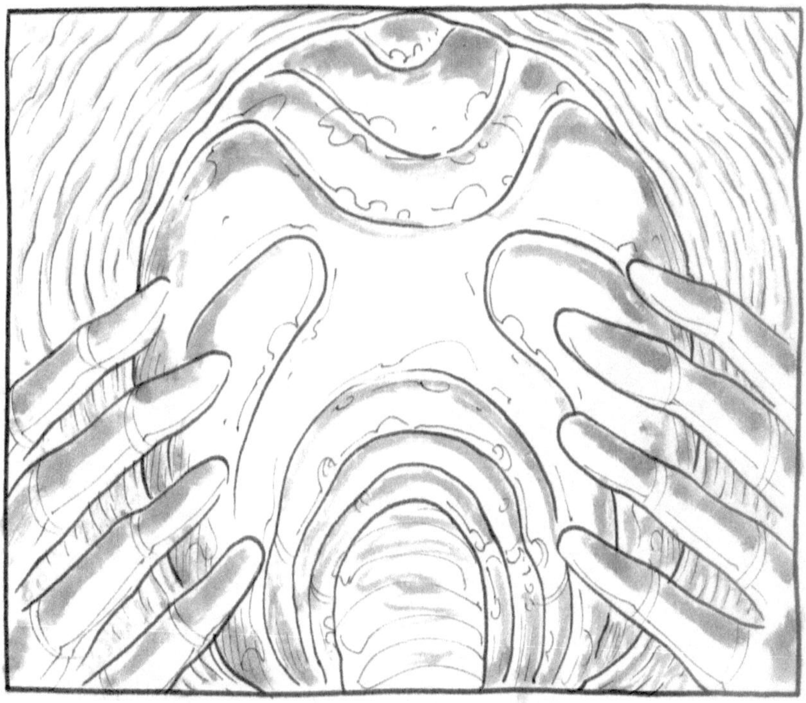

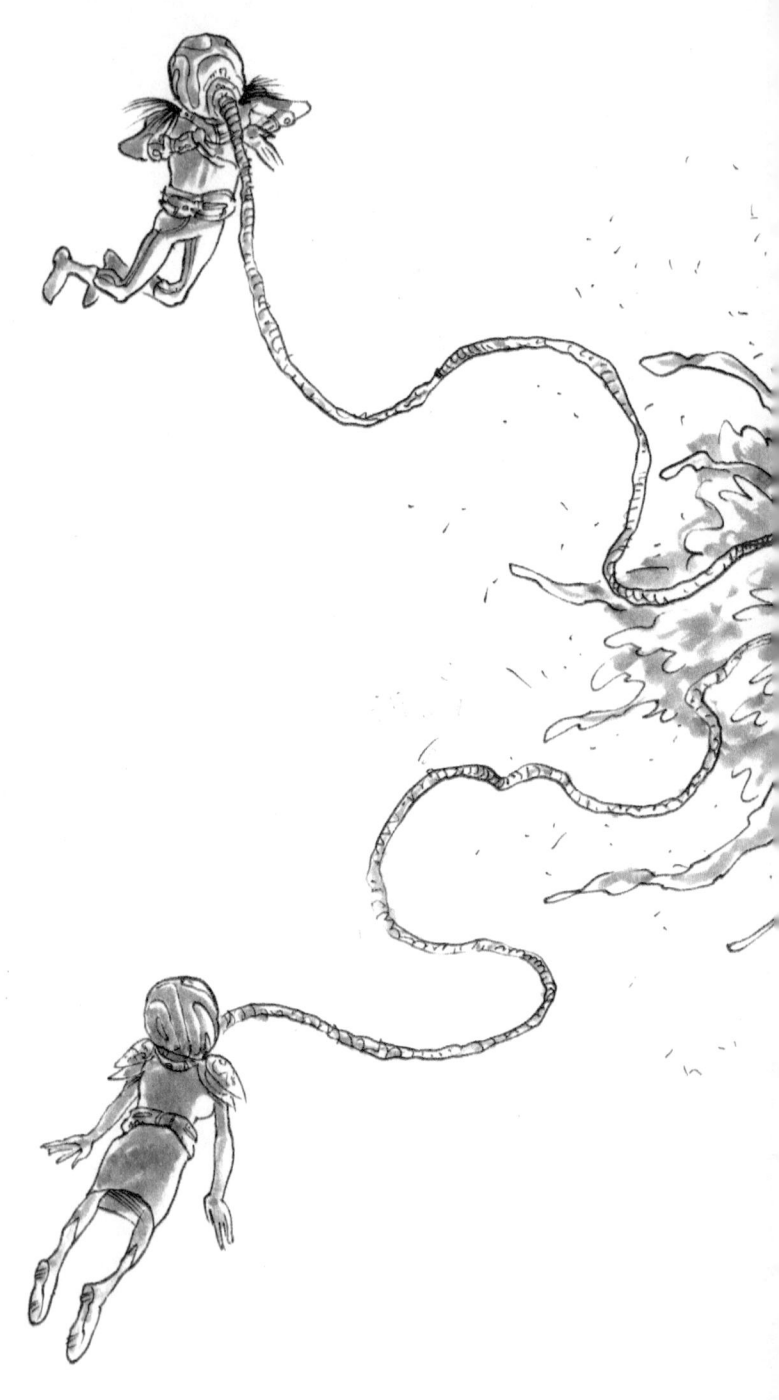

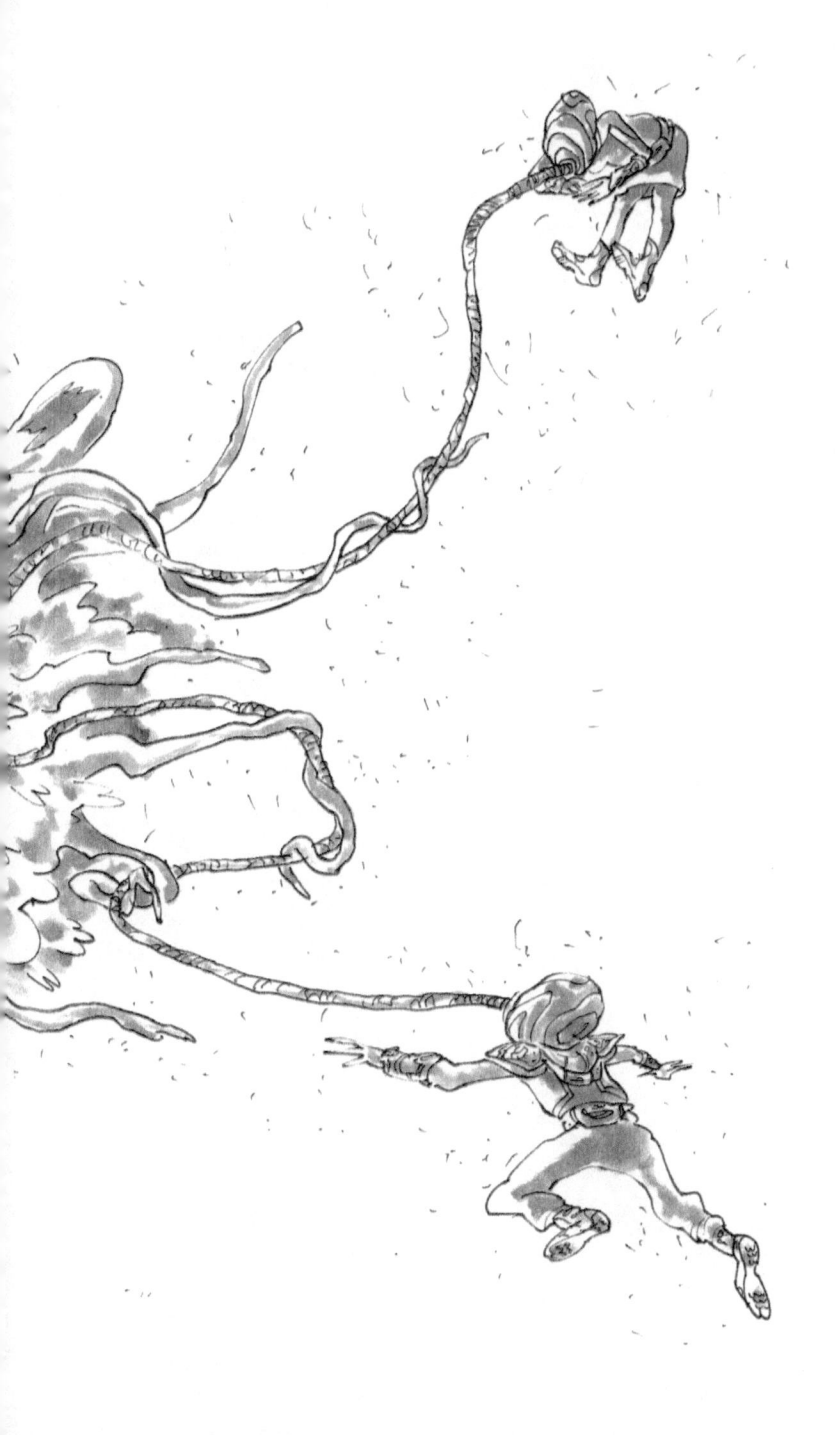

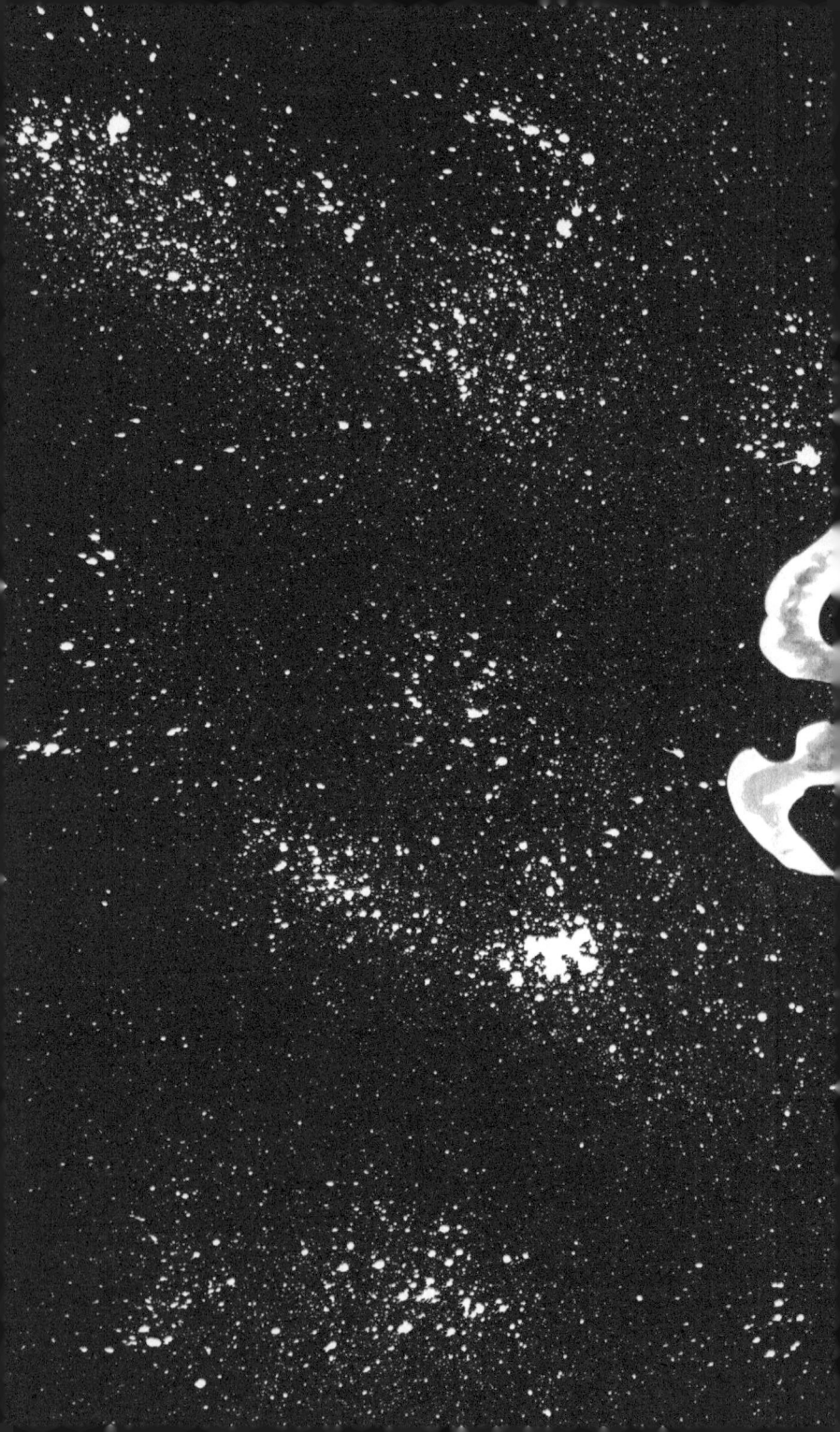

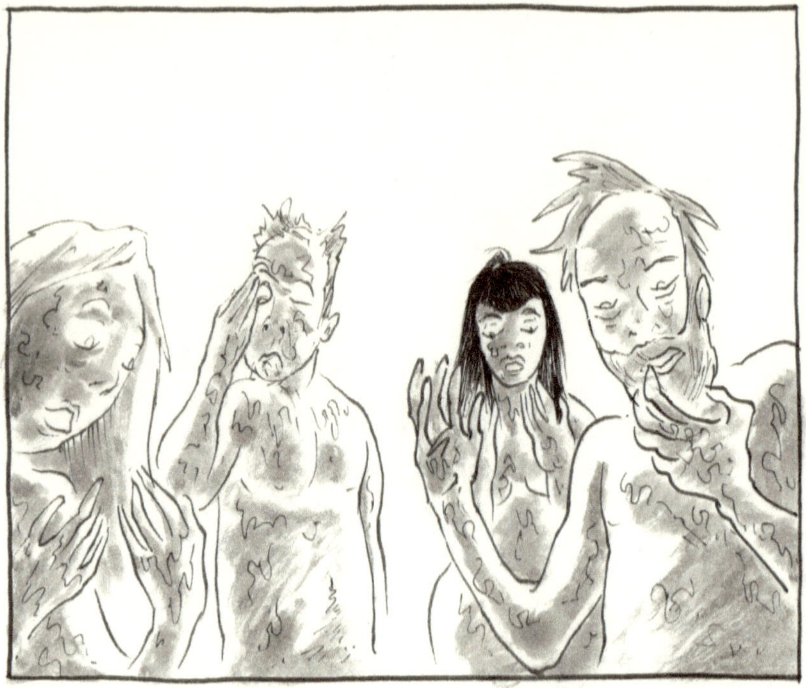
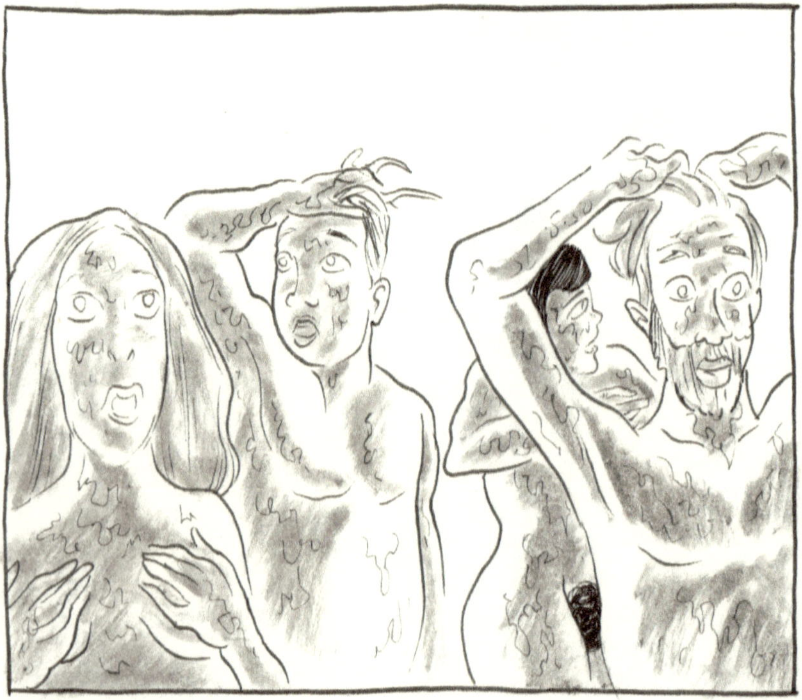

SNIP

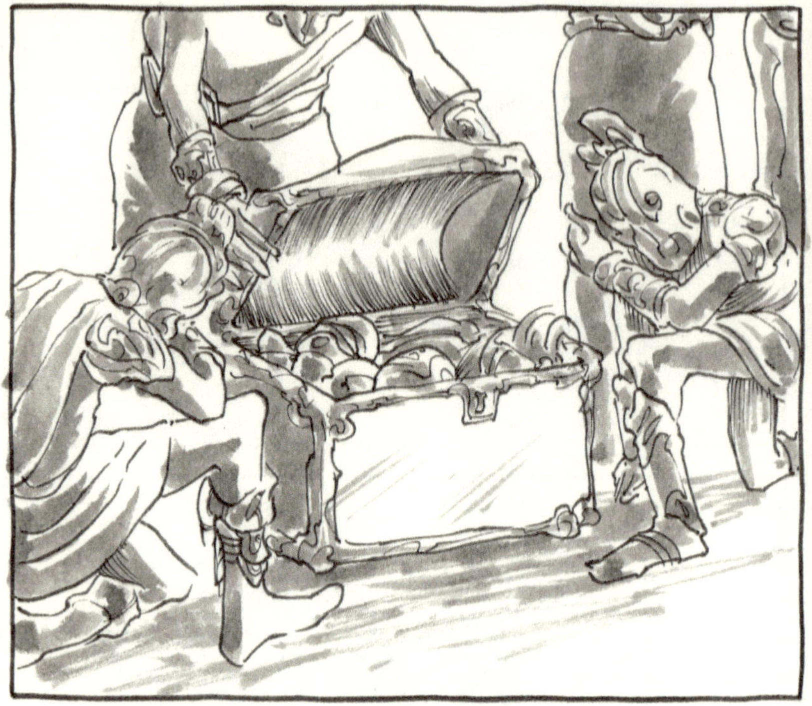

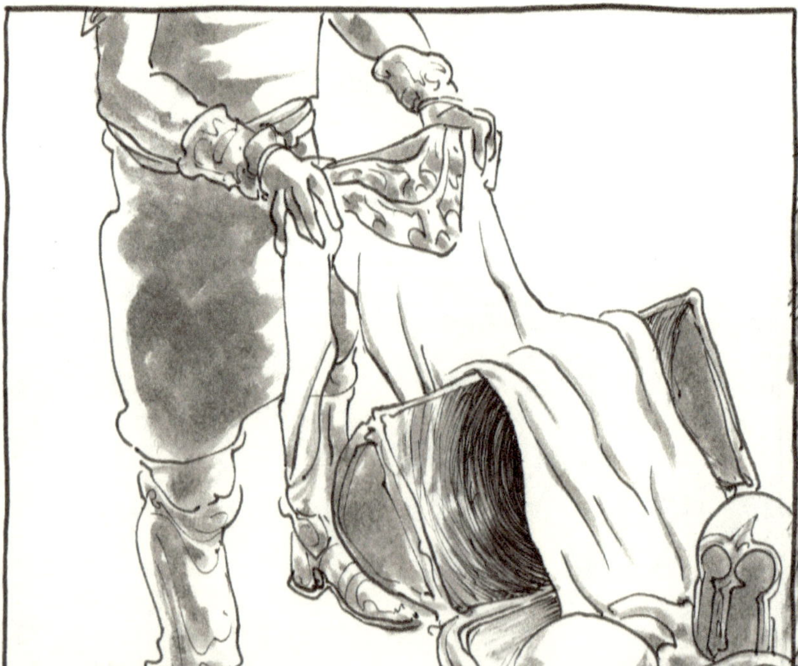

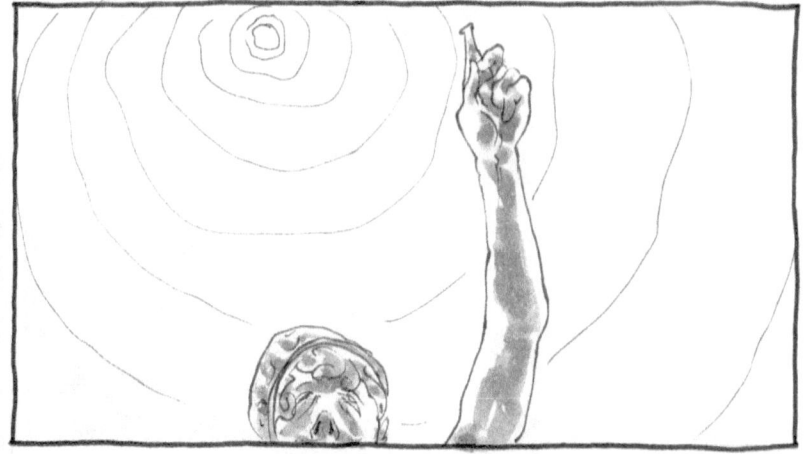

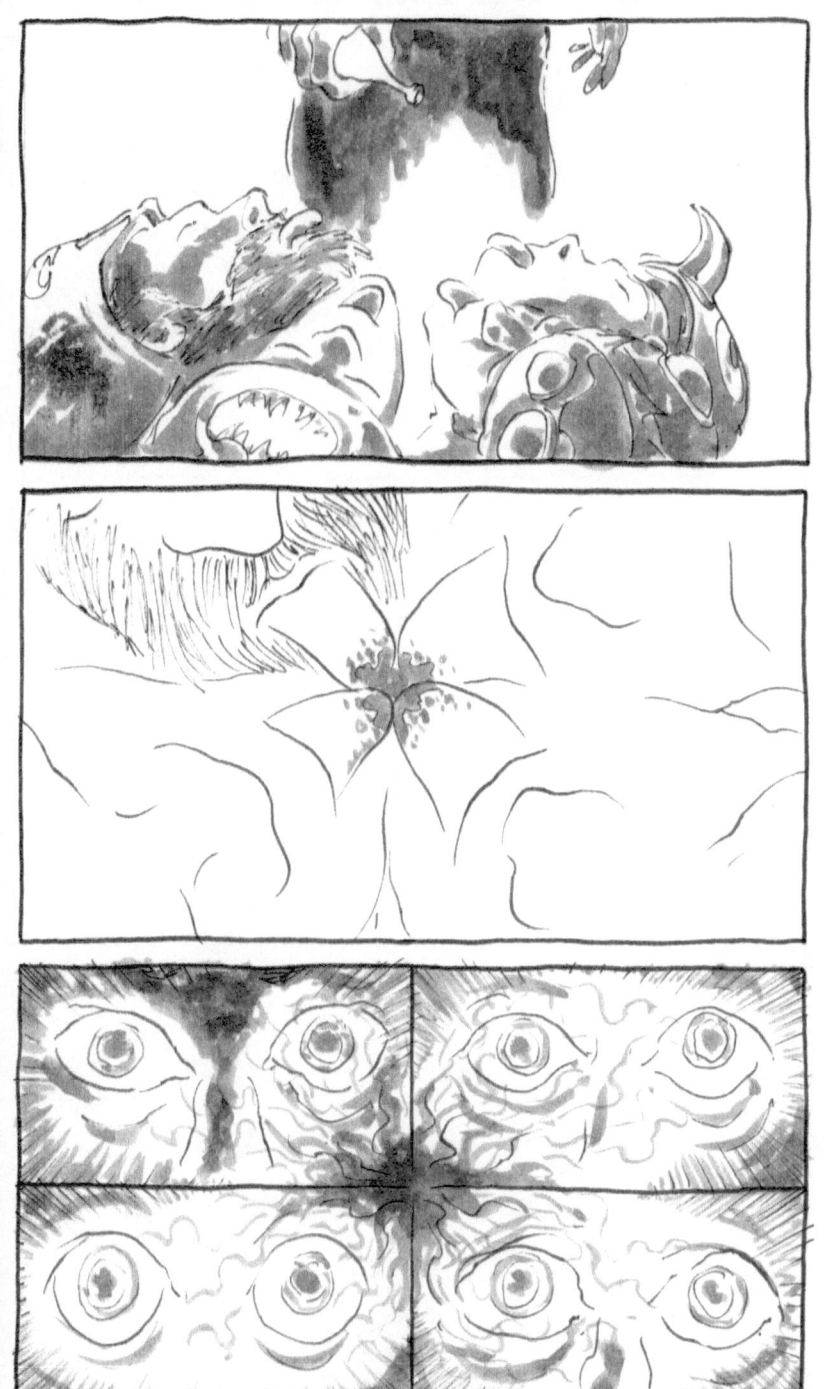

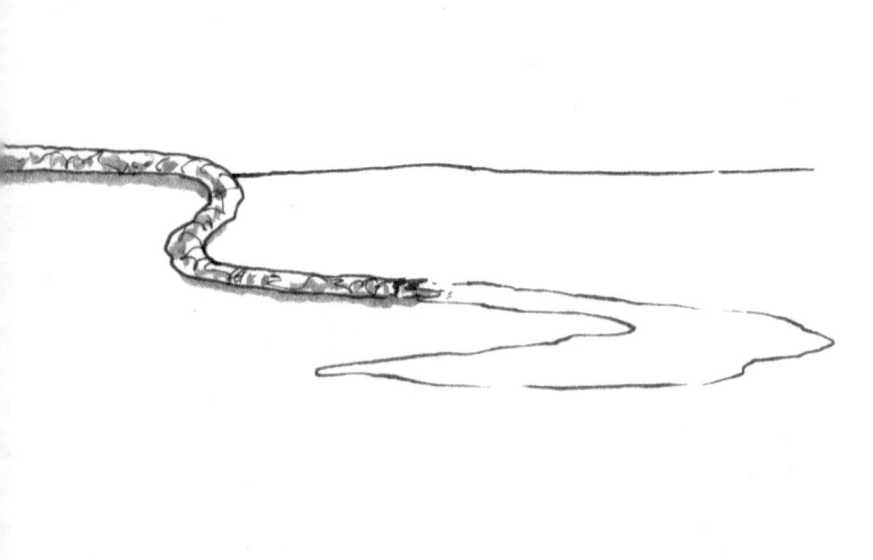

the end

## TRANSCENDENTAL SUPER-CONSCIOUS STATE

I HOPE I REACH A SUPER-CONSCIOUS STATE
WHERE I CAN BEND BOTH TIME AND SPACE
WHERE TIME IS SOMETHING I CAN NEVER KNOW
AND NO ONE CAN SEE WHERE I GO
AMEN, THE PRAYER WOULD END
MY MIND IS ALIGNED WITH EACH SIGN IN THE SKY
GOOD LUCK AND GODSPEED

## NOT TONIGHT

WELL THE LIGHTS, THEY WERE FLASHING
AND THE SMOKE GOT IN MY EYES
I TOOK YOUR HAND AND I SPUN YOU LIGHTLY
WE DRIFTED ON FORBIDDEN BEATS
SPUN FOREVER, BUT STILL STAYED ON OUR FEET
CAN I TAKE YOU HOME? NOT TONIGHT
SPILLED MY DRINK, STEPPED ON YOUR TOES
THE BEAT PLAYED ON, I FOLLOW WHERE IT GOES
AND WE SWAYED, BARELY IN TIME
AND WE MOANED A GOSPEL MOAN
OUR HANDS DRIFTED ON TO PARTS UNKNOWN
CAN I TAKE YOU HOME? NOT TONIGHT
MY WHISKEY BREATH, HOT IN YOUR EAR
FINGERS FUMBLED, COULDN'T HELP BUT TUG YOUR HAIR
THE DARK OF NIGHT WAS GROWING DIM
AND YOU TURNED AND YOU RAN RIGHT BACK TO HIM
MY NIGHT ENDED WHERE MY DIRTY THOUGHTS BEGAN
CAN I TAKE YOU HOME? NOT NEVER, NOT TONIGHT

## ALL THE LOVE

ITS GETTING LATE, AND I CAN ALMOST SEE THE LIGHT
I DROVE ALL NIGHT, TOWARDS A STEEL BLUE SKY
I GOTTA SPEED AND WEAVE AND FLY
FEEL A PUSH, AND ALL I DO IS SAY GOODBYE
SING YOUR NAME TO THE STEEL BLUE SKY,
KISS YOUR HEAD AND CLOSE YOUR EYES
SING YOUR NAME WITH A SHAKY VOICE,
WISH IT WENT DIFFERENT, IT AINT MY CHOICE
NO NO NO

LEAVE   YOUR   COAT   ON   YOU   CAN   STAY   OUTSIDE
SAYING   WHAT   YOU   SAY   WON'T   BE   DENIED
W               H                     O                    A
I HEARD WHAT YOU DONE AND THE THINGS THEY FOUND
YOU BETTER STOP YOUR LYING AND YOUR MESSIN AROUND
W               H                     O                    A
I KNOW YOU'RE COLD AND WHAT YOU DONE WAS TOO
I GOT BETTER THINGS TO DO THAN TALK TO YOU
W               H                     O                    A
LEAVE YOUR COAT ON CAUSE YOU AINT GONNA COME INSIDE
TAKE   YOUR   COAT   OFF   YOU   BETTER   EXPLAIN
GET YOUR STORY STRAIGHT CAUSE IT SOUNDS INSANE
W               H                     O                    A
SLOW   IT   ALL   DOWN   CAUSE   I   FEEL   CONFUSED
YOU'RE TWISTING MY WORDS AND I'M FEELING USED
W               H                     O                    A
I DON'T KNOW WHERE YOU'VE BEEN AND WHAT YOU'VE SEEN
YOU USED TO BE SWEET NOW YOU'RE DIRTY AND MEAN
W               H                     O                    A
THE   ORANGE   LIGHT,   THE   CITY   LIGHT,
THE   ONLY   LIGHT   I'LL   EVER   KNOW
NOT A LIGHT FROM ABOVE, THATS A LOVE I'LL NEVER SEE

I   DON'T   CARE   WHAT   HAPPENS   TO   THIS   WORLD
AS   LONG   AS   IT   HURTS
LONG   AS   ITS   MADE   TO   CRY
LONG   AS   IT   HURTS
I'VE DONE TOO MUCH LIVING FOR THIS WORLD
I   KNOW   THAT   IT   HURTS
KNOW   THAT   IT   MAKES   YOU   CRY
KNOW   THAT   IT   HURTS
ALL   OF   OUR   ACCOLADES
ARE   VERY   SHORT-LIVED
ALL   OF   OUR   VICTORIES
ARE   DUST   WITHIN   THE   WIND
ALL   OF   OUR   ACCOLADES
ARE   VERY   SHORT-LIVED
ALL   OF   OUR   VICTORIES
ARE   DUST   WITHIN   THE   WIND
DUST   IN   THE   WIND

## EDGE OF THE WORLD

LET GO OF YOUR ASHES IN THE AUTUMN WIND
OVER THE OCEAN WHEN THE TIDE CAME IN
AND RIGHT BACK OUT TO THE EDGE OF THE WORLD
I'M HOPING TO SEE YOU SOME TIME AGAIN
HOPING TO SEE YOU
THOUGH I KNOW I NEVER WILL

## LAST DAY

ON THE LAST DAY OF MY LIFE
I'M GONNA DANCE IN THE MOONLIGHT
I'LL TAKE MY TIME, LIGHT UP THAT FUNERAL PYRE
SAY A FEW WORDS, THEN CLIMB INSIDE
LET MY ASHES FLY, PLEASE DON'T CRY
LAY ME ON DOWN
DIG A BIG HOLE IN THE GROUND
LAY ME ON DOWN
AND I'LL LAY MYSELF TO SLEEP

## KISS THE DIRT

THE FIRES ARE THE ROADMAPS
HOW FAR BETWEEN THOSE DOTS OF LIGHT
IT HAPPENED ONCE BEFORE
ITS HAPPENING RIGHT NOW
I NAMED A LOT OF STARS
BUT I NEVER NAMED THE SUN
SO DO YOU THINK IT KNOWS, LIKE I KNOW
I KISSED THE SKY, BURNED MY LIPS
KISSED THE DIRT, LET IT HURT
THOSE LIGHTS ARE TOO FAR OFF
AND THATS WHY I NEARLY LOST MY WAY
WHAT WE SEE RIGHT NOW
ARE GHOSTS THAT BURNED OUT YESTERDAY
I'M LYING VERY STILL
AS THE BRIGHTNESS OF EACH FIRE MOVES AWAY
SO DO YOU THINK IT KNOWS, LIKE I KNOW
I KISSED THE SKY, BURNED MY LIPS
KISSED THE DIRT, LET IT HURT

## SERVANTS OF TWILIGHT

I CLENCH MY TEETH I KNOW
THE WORLD IT AINT GOT LONG
I FORGOT ALL I KNEW, I STARE AT THE SETTING SUN
MY BIRTH WAS NOT MY CHOICE, IN FACT IT WAS A FOLLY
I WALK ON EVERY DAY,
I WALK WITH YOU IN TWILIGHT, TWILIGHT, IN TWILIGHT,
DARKNESS, IN DARKNESS,
I LOOK TO THE SETTING SUN
I CLENCH MY TEETH I TASTE
THE ASH LEFT OF THE PLANET
I FORGOT ALL I KNEW, BURNED UP IN THE SETTING SUN
MY BIRTH WAS NOT MY CHOICE, IN FACT IT WAS A FOLLY
I WALK ON EVERY DAY,
I WALK WITH YOU IN TWILIGHT, TWILIGHT, IN TWILIGHT,
IN DARKNESS, IN DARKNESS
I LOOK TO THE SETTING SUN
IN DARKNESS, IN DARKNESS, IN DARKNESS

## REBORN

ALL I SEE ARE MOUNTAINS
ALL I SEE IS SAND
AND ITS ALWAYS BEEN THERE
FROM WHAT I UNDERSTAND
EVERYONE'S A COWARD, EVERYONE'S AFRAID
CAUSE THEY KNOW WHAT HAPPENS
WHEN YOUR BEST PLANS ARE LAID
WHEN I DIE I WILL BE DRUNK
CAUSE IN THAT FIRE I'LL BE REBORN
AND I WANNA HELP IT BURN
ALL MY FRIENDS ARE WITCHES
THAT THEY COULD NOT BURN
WHAT THEY DID NOT REALIZE
IS WE ALL GET OUR TURN
IF YOU THINK YOU OWN THIS
WATCH IT SLIP AWAY
IT DON'T BELONG TO NO ONE
IF IT DID YOU THINK THEY'D STAY
WHEN I DIE I WILL BE DRUNK
CAUSE IN THAT FIRE I'LL BE REBORN
AND I WANNA HELP IT BURN

☐ **DESCENDER by Descender** (ALR 001)
6 song debut EP. Available formats: Digipak CD, digital / streaming
90's Influenced post-hardcore. RIYL: Snapcase, Helmet, Quicksand

*"Angularly aggressive hardcore that takes an abrasive shape on purpose."* – CMJ

☐ **AND SO WE MARCHED by Descender** (ALR 002)
4 song EP. Available formats: Printed book, digital / streaming
90's Influenced post-hardcore. RIYL: Snapcase, Helmet, Quicksand

*"...a 21st Century compliant post-hardcore band that was raised on metal and got dosed with a tab of AmRep..."* – Jaded Scenster

☐ **TAKING DRUGS TO MAKE MUSIC TO SELL CARS TO** (ALR 003)
**by Human Highlight Reel**
4 song debut EP. Available formats: Vinyl record, printed book, digital / streaming
Instrumental post-rock. RIYL: Maserati, June of 44, Russian Circles

*"Aces instrumental post rock. Think Russian Circles or perhaps a more metal Seam..."*
– Jaded Scenster

☐ **JUDGE by Vagina Panther** (ALR 004)
5 song EP. Available formats: Printed book, digital / streaming
Heavy female-fronted garage rock. RIYL: QOTSA, Cheeseburger, Fu Manchu, Stooges

*"Vagina Panther rocks."* – Billboard

☐ **BLACK BLACK BLACK by Black Black Black** (ALR 005)
12 song debut LP. Available formats: Vinyl record, printed book, digital / streaming
Melodic death rock. RIYL: Akimbo, Torche, Lungfish, Black Flag

*"Brooklyn-by-way-of-Ohio doomsters offer up a big, nasty salute to gas tanks and goat hooves. It all coalesces to form one ravaging feast of melodic death rock that will satiate all your salacious needs, be it Nether-deity worshiping or rock star living."* – Broken Beard

☐ **GODMAKER by Godmaker** (ALR 007)
4 song debut LP. Available formats: Vinyl record, printed book, digital / streaming
Doomy sludge metal. RIYL: High on Fire, Red Fang, Mastodon, The Sword

*"An example of genuine out of-nowhere brilliance. A patient drawn out campaign of aggression."* – Relix

☐ **THE SPACE MERCHANTS by The Space Merchants** (ALR 008)
8 song debut LP. Available formats: Printed book, digital / streaming
Whiskey-soaked space-rock. RIYL: Black Mountain, Dead Meadow, The Besnard Lakes

*"A unique brand of lo-fi psych rock... their huge-yet-minimal sound, mixing psych with blues and country style riffs to make something great."* – Magnet

☐ **HIRAM-MAXIM by Hiram-Maxim** (ALR 009)

4 song debut LP. Available formats: Vinyl record, printed book, digital / streaming
Noisy experimental doomgaze. RIYL: Swans, Suicide, Pink Floyd, Oxbow

*"Builds into an apocalyptic fervor before dissipating into a cloudy haze & ending before you've had your fill."* – VICE

☐ **ALTERED STATES OF DEATH AND GRACE by Black Black Black** (ALR 010)

10 song sophomore LP. Available formats: Vinyl record, printed book, digital / streaming
Melodic death rock. RIYL: Akimbo, Torche, Lungfish, Black Flag

*"...the kind of good-natured misanthropy of bands like Whores or KEN mode, but the musical gestures beneath the noisy exterior are all forward-charging, Kyuss-worshipping sludge n' roll. It's basically underground metal's version of a radio banger."* – BrooklynVegan

☐ **TRESPASSES by Nathaniel Shannon & The Vanishing Twin** (ALR 011)

15 song debut LP. Available formats: Printed book, digital / streaming
Unsettling bedroom recording darkness. RIYL: Lanegan, Badalemnti, Springsteen, Waits

*"Shannon's spoken word-style vocals over haunting and minimalist instrumentals lend a creepy atmosphere to the record."* – Decibel

☐ **FERA by Husbandry** (ALR 012)

8 song debut LP. Available formats: Printed book, CD, digital / streaming
Female-fronted math rock meets post-hardcore. RIYL: Mars Volta, Glassjaw, Refused, Deftones

*"It's hard to believe that Husbandry is not the biggest band in the world. They're heavy and mathy, chaos wrapped in hard rock and heavy metal."* – Nerdist

☐ **MURDEREDMAN by MURDEREDMAN** (ALR 013)

8 song sophomore LP. Available formats: Vinyl record, printed book, digital / streaming
Post-punk inspired noise rock. RIYL: Savages, Bauhaus, Boris, Killing Joke

*"A patient and disciplined examination of anxiety and melancholy underpinned with a cathartic tension-and-release structure that borrows from goth, post-metal, and no-wave..."* – New Noise Magazine

☐ **IN TENSIONS by Lo-Pan** (ALR 014)

5 song EP. Available formats: Vinyl record, printed book, CD, digital / streaming
Anthemic desert rock. RIYL: Soundgarden, ASG, Torche, Red Fang

*"Calling Lo-Pan a stoner band is a disservice to the amalgam of influences the band successfully merges together: the soulful alt rock of the 90s with a thundering doom/sludge sound that's equal parts immediate and timeless."* – Nine Circles

☐ **GHOSTS by Hiram-Maxim** (ALR 015)

7 song sophomore LP. Available formats: Vinyl record, printed book, digital / streaming
Noisy experimental doomgaze. RIYL: Swans, Suicide, Pink Floyd, Oxbow

*"Everything is awash in mesmerizing ambient skree and squalls of atonal feedback. Think an extended, updated version of side 2 of Black Flag's My War."* – Hellride Music

☐ **BAD WEEDS NEVER DIE by Husbandry** (ALR 017)

5 song EP. Available formats: Printed book, CD, digital / streaming
Female-fronted math rock meets post-hardcore. RIYL: Mars Volta, Glassjaw, Refused, Deftones

*"Brooklyn's Husbandry sound like a faster, more aggressive Mars Volta, delivering soaring vocals and excellent musicianship in densely packed songs that constantly surprise."* – Echoes and Dust

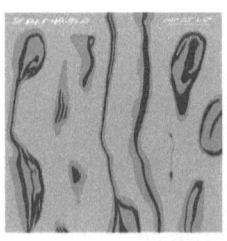

The music for this release
can be downloaded
via the link below:

http://aqualamb.org/016

www.ingramcontent.com/pod-product-compliance
Lightning Source LLC
Chambersburg PA
CBHW021930170626
46807CB00007B/3045